Dazzlers

Elanaaga

Ukiyoto Publishing

To my close friend, Dr. D. Narayana (Dubai).

Contents

Living Corpse

Despite having eyes
 I can't see beautiful things
Though I have ears
 I can't listen to sweet notes
 I have a heart
 But no feelings are born in it
 Isn't a corpse better than me?

Realisation

Having become affluent

I tasted all the luxuries

But spending a day with a pauper

who is a paragon of virtue

I realised I'm the poorest

The Change

I ran with a sword in my hand

to chop off the head of a haughty man

But moved by his affectionate smile

offered him flowers,

fell prostrate before his feet

and returned.

The Fleeting Joy

I was puffed up with joy
when I reached the land's surface
from a deep gorge,
but soon saddened realising
I've to climb a mountain.

Obtrusion

Pushing aside the purport
some words rush obtrusively
to the front in poetry;
Always, such knowledge
should be present in the poet's mind.

Sensitive Countenance

He exulted that he has
the fairest complexion
in the whole class.
But when a fairer boy joined,
his face "grew dark."

Quantity - Quality

Trumpeted a poet thus:
"I penned piles of books."
Quality, not quantity is that counts,
he should realize.

Disillusionment

Want of prosperity is a pebble,

lack of satisfaction is a big mountain.

Fortune of creativity is the sun;

content of comforts material,

merely a candlelight.

The Effect

When he was a gardener,

jasmines blossomed in his breath.

But when he became a clerk in a club

only the stink of currency prevailed!

Manifestation

Sitting in a closed room,

I opened a newspaper.

The outside world

Lay spread before me.

Miss Fortune

Grief-stricken he was,

for he didn't have ladders

As the good time came now he got one.

But can't use it

since he is bed-ridden

Absurdity

When a dull head moves

in a brand new Benz car

all heads turn to it

But no head cares to glance at

a mountain of erudition

riding on a rickety scooter

This is but an incident common

Stance – Success

My enemy roared like a tiger,

sprang up like a lion.

Intrepid, I was.

But later when he

Maintained a serious calm

I trembled with fear

The Bigger Test

I finished taking my exam

Now preparing for even a bigger test

What's it?

Waiting for the results

Of the exam!

'Like - All' Syndrome

Disconcerted I am

when I see the crop of 'likes' on Facebook

Nothing is dislikeable!

Isn't this an enigma uncrackable?

Time Teaches

Until responsibilities frightened me
I didn't realise the value of childhood
Until I lost my way in the deep woods
I didn't recognize the delight of the backyard

Only when a flame singes
snow's worth is known perhaps

Pain – Pleasure

Disgusted I am;
Win after a win befell me.
Distressed I am
For defeat has eluded me

Misery, perhaps
is better than painful pleasures

Felicitous Felicitation

The desert that

daringly dreams dense clouds

deserves felicitation with

wreaths of raindrops

Intrinsic

Personalities determine people

One who adores dagger
doesn't like compassion
The other who rears rabbits
detests cruelty

Unguessable

When the moon is hiding behind clouds

we can know it

But sometimes can't surmise

what is behind someone's words

Right Remedy

Of late, the whole world is
appearing black to me
People, environs - everything
is dark around me

I pondered a lot
and chose the right remedy:
Wash out the murk
accumulated inside me

Incompatibility

His heart is soft as butter

but sharp as a knife

The knife cannot soften

Nor can it incarnate as butter

The result, alas, is -

He is fighting against himself daily

Delectation

The song is the Ganges

Raga is a raft

Notes are boons

And the journey is joyful

Aberrance

When I led a pauper's life

I only wanted food, nothing more.

Now, I have enough food

and lo, my heart is hankering for a bike!

Sacred Sobs

Whenever I read sublime poetry, I cried
Whenever I listened to great music, I wept
Whenever I came across humanity personified,
 I whimpered

After so many wailings
 how sanctified has my heart become!

Effort – Effect

Where a gun is buried

there sprouts a tree of bullets.

Sprinkle seeds of love

in your heart's field, my friend.

Affection grows abundantly

The Mellowing

He raved like an enraged bull

in the streets of the town.

On reaching home

kids greeted warmly

At once, his stony heart

melted like ice!

The Core Commodity

Words are only outer sheaths
 in poetry
True, struggle we should, for them.
But nothing is more vital than
the core ingredient

No poetry can germinate
in dried up heart

Disgruntlement

Making language a thread
I stringed words, made garlands of poems
They became fragrant lines
But words, not well-fitted
became hissing sentences
and sprang up to bite me

Attempt – Result

Sweet notes are secreted

only when bamboos are wounded

Seeds bring out the oil

only on being battered

Rigorous toil

is required for good results

Protective Covering

If you compliment him

he just smiles

If you criticize him

he just smiles

If you berate him

he just smiles

If you beat him

he just smiles

A smile had been the strong corset

that had been protecting his inner self

from bouquets and brickbats

Perception

Sweet *ragas* can't emanate from
flutes made of gold
Rose petals can't come in handy
for cooking any curry

Monetary values
mar man's perception

Disparity

This is a world of disparities
Here, a big fish that engulfs a smaller one
is itself devoured by a still bigger one
In the same way, a tall fellow
is outwitted by a taller one
Everyone has to put effort,
inch forward in stages
and try to touch the sky

Concealment

An ocean looks tranquil
it may be concealing volcanoes though;
Some people look unperturbed
bombshells are bursting inside though

No gauge is there
that can measure
internal devastation

Bane – Boon

If life has to depend
on wages, it is a tragedy
Strengthening by affection
rather than by affluence
is the real prosperity

Variance

Heart treads on a footpath
while the brain travels on clouds

One is great
The other is good

Dwellings - Their Roles

Staying in own house for long
one feels like going to farm-house
But, unable to continue there
wants to reach home

Poetry, to me, is own house
while translation is a farm-house

But, of late
they've exchanged their roles

Distinction

A bird flying in the skyway is not great

for it has wings

A kite floating in firmament

is also not great

because it has a string attached

A cracker shooting into the welkin

is not amazing either

since it has gunpowder inside

An aeroplane flying high above

is not a miracle too

for it does so with the power of fuel

But a poet's imagination

touching the sky is indeed great

Because unaided it is

in achieving the feat

Fortune Of Forty Winks

Trying to sleep on a soft mattress
in an AC room, unsuccessful I was.

Jealousy is what I was left with
when I saw poor people
sleeping like logs on hard soil

The Great Destroyer

Nothing is more destructive than a tongue

A single sentence
can wreak havoc in many a heart
One utterance is enough
to cause upheaval

Different Discernment

When I see India that entered America

I am pleased greatly

But on seeing America

that infiltrated India

I feel melancholy

One is a sign of our gumption

while the other

puts our culture to destruction

Fortune Of Harmony

Belittling a noun

an adjective boasted:

"Your furtherance only lies in me"

The noun went underground

didn't return for years

The adjective sat sullenly

and contemplated:

"Only with a noun I've glory

Only with a noun, I've integrity"

Power Of Place

Eight cyphers stood in a row

to the left of digit one

The latter taunted the zeros:

"Only in me lies your existence.

Without me your value has insignificance"

The cyphers discussed

and migrated to right from left

Now,

digit one has nothing left

except to become long faced

Experience – Consequence

An article was sent to a magazine
for appraisal and publication
The magazine did not print it
 kept in abeyance for long
 Had the article stayed at its creator
 it would have got daily attention
 Languished for long without care
 it came back after many months
 Its creator lamented
 Attended it every day
 The article started shining with a gleam
 but refused to go to a new magazine

Benefit Of Being Old

I, who cannot pass a password test
dreamt of old times sans passwords

In those old times
passes were many, failures were few

Brilliance – Belittlement

A thick book cover

always talks disparagingly

about an inner page

But, the inner page might contain

profound matter

The book cover's glitters

are tinsel's superficial glints

Superficial Shine

A coronet laughed at shoes mockingly

But, coronet hasn't much use in reality

Shoes are very useful, aren't they?

Eminence

True it is

that bus is faster than pedestrian

a train than a bus, plain than train

and spacecraft than a plane.

But, it's only a pedestrian

who can move with no

immediate requirement of fuel

Dampness Does The Wonder

Profound poetry cannot take birth
without drizzle in the heart
A blistering bosom cannot become wet
with words that are not moist

Facebook – A Real Hook

Once bitten by the bug of Facebook,
your brain will start falling sick.
No rest will be gotten even for one day,
peace of the brain will always be at bay.

Sham Straight Shooters

Some people furiously tell
anger indeed is very bad!
Poor fellows, they're blind
to their defect, it's sad.

Grades

Some are have-nots who cannot
enter (invest thousands of rupees) in
                              business.
Some others may invest thousands of bucks
but cannot get back even hundreds

Hype – Fallout

I considered myself a great poet,
  made others say the same.
  Forty years later,
  my name faded into oblivion;
that of another who wrote
better but remained calm
shined brightly.

Words – Value

I sieved a bowl of words,

picked a handful from them

for penning a poem.

The poem came off nicely

I haven't thrown away

the remaining words.

They fitted well in a poem

that I wrote the next day!

No word can be discarded

forever, perhaps!

Poetry – Poet

Poetry is a festoon

of charming reflections

A poet wages war

against unpleasant ideations

He, thus,

epitomises beauty

on all occasions

Premature Poem

A poetic thought should keep growing

as a foetus in the womb of a pen.

Only when fully grown

it should take birth.

Babies born before full term

are premature and often weak

The Miser

I like that miserly poet the most;

am a bit jealous, too.

He gets more benefits by spending less

While I spend more and gain less

Why should we spend more?

The words, I mean.

Circle

Seeing the fortnights
of light and darkness,
we should press the
chequered life to heart.
The snow on the Himalayas
accumulates in winter
and melts in summer

Encroachment

Encroaching upon the wall,

a diehard politician

evicted a cat.

The feline felt shy

The Pain Of Heaviness

It is difficult to describe the pain
>   Of the clouds that did not rain.
>   Those that rained are fortunate;
>   Reducing the heaviness of others
>   Is not as easy as we contemplate.

Haystack

Wearied I am
With the search for a needle
In this haystack.

Frightening repulsive pictures,
Short stubs of strings resembling one-liners,
Dry coconuts devoid of water inside –
All have accumulated in this haystack
Making the search difficult

Yet, I don't feel like stopping.
A faint hope that the needle
Might be found lingers around!

***

The Age Of Shackles

The invisible hand that ties
inner instinct with a tether
disquiets mind greatly.

Shackles of subject selection for poets,
fetters of faith for spirited thinkers,
those of bigotry for the men of maturity…

I have to break my shackles

When will good times come?
When would people be free from shackles?

***

Weariness

I, journeying in the hot sun
of a mid-afternoon outside the town…

Tall toddy trees are there,
 but how much shade can they offer?
While I was gasping, oozing sweat,
 a small mango tree invited me affectionately.

Some comforter is always there in this world

Resting in the cool shade,
I looked at the toddy trees.

*****

External Charm

With a stone-built wall around it,
a well is attracting the onlookers.

Smooth cement floor, beautiful plants
adorned its surroundings.
Its graceful pulley is causing ecstasy

People are coming in hordes
to see the famous well.

But the well dried up long ago!

***

Discrepancy

Different people have

Different yardsticks.

Even one person's benchmark

might vary with time.

Breaking the mystery

of yardsticks is a big challenge.

New Truth

Catching a mouse
digging a hill is not folly
when the mouse caught
is exceptional, though tiny.

Defect

I employed partly known words

In my poem.

I know not their nature fully.

Therefore,

The poem lacked the feeling

Trouble

Discrimination is a snake,

discretion a frog.

The frog is angered

if the snake is asked to bite.

The serpent is enraged

if asked to give up!

***

Apathy – After Effect

The nonchalance of Dhritarashtra
In front of wailing Draupadi
Is the seed of forest fire,
Which would burn Kauravas.

Roots Of Charm

Grotesqueness doesn't disappear
if the mirror is banished.
Prettiness doesn't sprout
in soil sans the seed of beauty
even if watered.

The Outer Shine

Sitting on a head,
a tiara looked at an anklet
and sniggered.
Mortified, the latter walked out
emanating wonderful musical notes.

The crown danced demonically,
cherished the insult of the anklet.
But no music nor beauty
existed in its prance.

***

About the Author

Elanaaga

Elanaaga is a pen name. The author's actual name is Dr Surendra Nagaraju. He is a paediatrician, but is now fully into creative writing, translation, and criticism etc. He penned 33 books so far. Fifteen of them are original writings (mainly in Telugu language), while 18 are translations. Of the latter, 8 are from English to Telugu and 10 vice versa. Besides poetry and translations, he wrote books on language propriety, classical music etc. He rendered Latin American stories, African stories, Somerset Maugham's stories, and world stories and so on.